at the supermarket

Jean and Gareth Adamson

Blackie Children's Books

BLACKIE CHILDREN'S BOOKS

Published by the Penguin Group
Penguin Books Ltd, 27 Wrights Lane, London W8 5TZ, England
Penguin Books USA Inc., 375 Hudson Street, New York, NY 10014, USA
Penguin Books Australia Ltd, Ringwood, Victoria, Australia
Penguin Books Canada Ltd, 10 Alcorn Avenue, Toronto, Ontario, Canada M4V 3B2
Penguin Books (NZ) Ltd, 182-190 Wairau Road, Auckland 10, New Zealand

Penguin Books Ltd, Registered Offices: Harmondsworth, Middlesex, England

First published 1988 by Blackie Children's Books
This edition first published 1992
3 5 7 9 10 8 6 4 2

Copyright © 1988 by Jean and Gareth Adamson

The moral right of the author and illustrator has been asserted

Made and printed in Great Britain by William Clowes Limited, Beccles and London

A CIP catalogue record for this book is available from the British Library

ISBN 0 216 92858 3 Hbk
ISBN 0 216 92857 5 Pbk

Early one Saturday morning, Topsy
and Tim and Mummy and Dad set out
in their car. They were going to
do their shopping at the big
supermarket.

They drove into the supermarket
car park. Lots of other cars had
got there before them.

'There's a space!' shouted Topsy
and Tim both together.
'Well spotted,' said Mummy.
Dad parked the car carefully and
they all got out.

Inside the supermarket, there were
lots of trolleys on wheels. Mummy
chose one and Tim started to
push it for her.
'I want to push it,' said Topsy.
'I got it first,' said Tim.

'Steady on,' said Dad. 'We'll need two trolleys for all our shopping. You can help me push mine, Topsy.'

Mummy had brought a very long
shopping list with her. She
divided it into two pieces and
gave one piece to Dad.

Tim and Mummy went to get some fruit.
They got apples, bananas and pears.
Tim chose one orange for himself
and one for Topsy.

Dad looked at his shopping list.
'We need eggs, coffee, Cornflakes
and cat food,' he said.
While Dad was getting the Cornflakes,
Topsy went to find the cat food.
Dad didn't see her go.

Topsy soon found the shelves of cat and dog food. She chose the sort that Kitty liked best.

Topsy turned round and looked for Dad and his trolley—but Dad had disappeared.

The supermarket was full of people
pushing trolleys, but Topsy
couldn't see Dad anywhere.

Topsy felt lost and lonely and she began to cry. She looked for someone to help her. She knew she should only go to someone who worked in the shop—but who?
The lady behind the cheese counter looked friendly.
'My mummy and daddy have gone home without me,' Topsy told her.

'I'm sure they haven't,' said
the lady. She looked around and saw
a little boy wearing a T shirt
just like the one Topsy had on.
'Is that little boy your brother?'
she asked.
'It's Tim!' said Topsy.

Tim took Topsy back to Mummy
and Dad. Dad had been very worried.
'Where did you go, Topsy?' he
said. 'I thought I had lost you.'
He lifted Topsy up into the child's
seat on his trolley.
'I won't lose you again,' he said.
Topsy liked riding in Dad's trolley.

When Tim saw Topsy riding in Dad's
trolley, he wanted to ride too.
'Not now,' said Mummy. 'There's
too much shopping in my trolley
and we're nearly at the check-out.'

There were lots of sweets beside
the check-out. Tim was
just going to ask for some when
Mummy said, 'I've got a special
job for you, Tim. Please will you
find two big cardboard boxes to
put the shopping in.'

Tim found a huge pile of cardboard
boxes in one corner of the supermarket.
He pulled one out from the bottom
of the pile. Boxes came tumbling down
from the top and one landed on
Tim's head.

Topsy laughed when she saw it.
'You look like a spaceman,'
she said.

Mummy and Dad had got everything
on their lists. Now it was time
to pay for it. Topsy helped Dad
unload the shopping on to the
moving counter. The check-out lady
added up what it all cost.

Mummy paid for it and she and Tim packed it neatly into the big cardboard boxes, ready to take to the car.

Dad had one more job for Topsy
and Tim to do before they went
home. It was to ride in the
supermarket spaceship. Topsy
and Tim liked that job best of all.